T e One That ot Away

Published in 2010 by Evans Publishing Ltd,
 2A Portman Mansions,
Chiltern St, London WIU 6NR

© Evans Brothers Limited 2010

Editor: Su Swallow
Designer: D.R. Ink

British Library Cataloguing in Publication Data

Harrison, Paul, 1969-
   The one that got away. -- (Take 2)
   1. Children's stories.
   I. Title II. Series
   823.8'2-dc22

ISBN-13: 9780237542030

Printed in China.

The One That Got Away

Paul Harrison and Tim Archbold

Evans

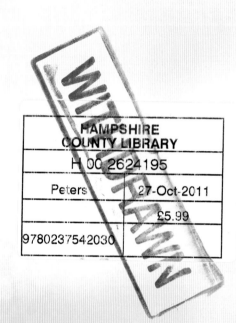

It was early. Akaka was
the only one awake.

Quietly, he grabbed his fishing pole and crept out. His family were always treating him like a baby, because he was the youngest. Well, today he would bring back the biggest fish they had ever seen.

It was cold outside. A scrunching in the snow behind him made Akaka jump, but it was only Amaraq, his dog.

"Hush now, Amaraq," said Akaka.
"This trip is not for you.

Fishing is about sitting and waiting and all you know is running and barking. Stay here."

Akaka set off over the hill to the frozen lake. Amaraq followed anyway, out of sight. An early walk is always an adventure for a dog.

Akaka was never allowed to go anywhere by himself. It was too dangerous, they said. "What could be dangerous about fishing?" thought Akaka.

He cut a hole in the
ice and waited.

Akaka did not know that Nanuq the ice
bear was watching, with a child-sized hole
in his stomach.

Nanuq padded softly across the snow.
Belly flat and quiet as a whisper he slid
across the ice.

Akaka felt a large fish
nibble at the bait.
"Easy now," he said to himself.
"No sudden moves."

Nanuq prepared to pounce.

Bark! Roar! Shock! Amaraq jumped
at Nanuq and Akaka fled, fast as the
wind, for home.

Amaraq was home before him, limping but happy.

Akaka's family were awake and waiting, too.

"Where have you been?"
they asked.

He dared not tell the
whole truth.

"Fishing," he replied. "I had one but it got away. It was huge."

His father looked at Amaraq and
the scrap of white fur in his jaws
and smiled.

"I'm sure you are right. But today I think you were the one that got away, my child."

If you enjoyed this book, look out for another Take 2 title:

the story of a dramatic sled dog race across 1000 miles of Alaska that takes place every year, called the Iditarod.